This book belongs to

. . . .

For my daughters, Emma and Maddie – TT

For Mum, Dad and Jacey – NP

First published in paperback in Great Britain by Digital Leaf in 2014

ISBN: 978-1-909428-19-5

www.digitalleaf.co.uk

digitalleaf

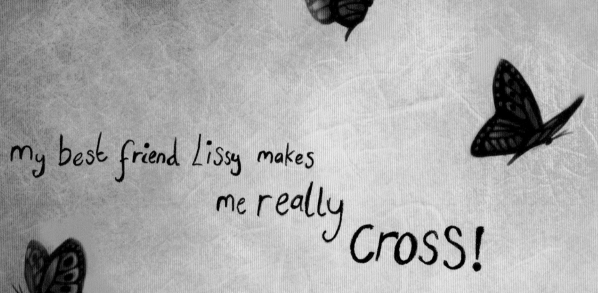

my best friend Lissy makes
me really
crosS!

Every time I say something,
She always says,

"So What!"

And do you know what my best friend Lissy said? She said...

Perhaps I should have said,

"Mummy bought me a camel with six humps..."

and she lets me ride it ten times
around the garden
before bedtime."

But I
didn't...

But she just said, in her most bored voice...

"Mummy bought me a long red velvet gown, a sparkly tiara and a real magic wand.

I could have said,

And she lets me wear them when I ride my camel with six humps ten times around the garden **before bedtime!**"

But I didn't...

The next day I was
off school sick,

and on Wednesday morning I told Lissy that I'd been in bed with a bad cold and cough.

But Lissy just screamed at the top of her voice...

Then Lissy left me with a
dreadful headache and went
off to play with Samantha.

She's never played with
Samantha before.

Lissy said she didn't
like Samantha.

That made
me **wish**
I'd said...

"A slimy alien landed in our garden while I was riding the camel with six humps and swapped my real magic wand and sparkly tiara for a rare disease from another planet."

And that I was alright now, even though the camel wasn't.

But I didn't.

So, on Friday, on the way home from school, I crossed my fingers behind my back and said to Lissy,

"Guess what! Mummy said that if the weather's nice tomorrow,

I'm allowed to dress up in my long red velvet gown, put on my sparkly tiara,

take my real magic wand and our pet camel with six humps (if the vet can cure him of the rare disease in time)

and go on a dinosaur hunt."

And do you know what Lissy said?

She said...

And then Lissy said something to me. She said,

"Well, I'm going to the park with Samantha!"

And do you know what I said? I said...